For Marigold

BEACH LANE BOOKS • An imprint of Simon & Schuster Children's Publishing Division • 1230 Avenue of the Americas. New York. New York 10020 • © 2021 by Alison Lester • Originally published in Australia in 2021 by Allen & Unwin • Book design by Lauren Rille © 2023 by Simon & Schuster. Inc. • All rights reserved. including the right of reproduction in whole or in part in any form. • BEACH LANE BOOKS and colophon are trademarks of Simon & Schuster. Inc. • For information about special discounts for bulk purchases. please contact Simon & Schuster Special Sales at 1-866-506-1949 or business@simonandschuster.com. • The Simon & Schuster Speakers Bureau can bring authors to your live event. For more information or to book an event. contact the Simon & Schuster Speakers Bureau at 1-866-248-3049 or visit our website at www.simonspeakers .com. • The text for this book was set in Plumbsky. • Manufactured in China • 0822 SCP • First Beach Lane Books US edition January 2023 • 10 9 8 7 6 5 4 3 2 1 • Library of Congress Cataloging-in-Publication Data • Names: Lester. Alison. author. illustrator. • Title: Noni the pony counts to a million / Alison Lester. • Description: First edition. | New York : Beach Lane Books. 2022. | Series: Noni the pony | "First published in Australia in 2021 by Allen & Unwin" | Audience: Ages 0-8. | Audience: Grades K-1. | Summary: Noni the Pony counts everything from her two friends to the cars going by. all the way to a million stars in the night sky. • Identifiers: LCCN 2021056827 (print) | LCCN 2021056828 (ebook) | ISBN 9781665922289 (hardcover) | ISBN 9781665922296 (ebook) • Subjects: CYAC: Stories in rhyme. | Ponies-Fiction. | Animals-Fiction. | Counting-Fiction. | LCGFT: Stories in rhyme. | Picture books. • Classification: LCC PZ8.3.L54935 Np 2022 (print) | LCC PZ8.3.L54935 (ebook) | DDC [E]-dc23 • LC record available at https://lccn.loc.gov/2021056827 • LC ebook record available at https://lccn.loc.gov/2021056828

Alison Lester

noni the pony
counts to a million

BEACH LANE BOOKS · New York London Toronto Sydney New Delhi

Noni the Pony stands under **one** tree . . .

and watches her **two** friends
dance by the sea.

She gives **three** speckled hens
a ride up the hill.

Then races **four** cows
down to the mill.

Five wallaby pals
come hip-hopping by . . .

as **six** dusky wood swallows
swoop through the sky.

Seven stout puppies
play hide-and-seek.

And **eight** butterflies flutter over the creek.

Nine spotted fish
swim deep in the reeds.

And **ten** ladybugs
march over the weeds.

Noni's friend Helga
has **dozens** of spots.

And Great-Uncle Harry
has **hundreds** of dots.

Noni watches the lights
of **thousands** of cars.

Then sleeps through the night
under **millions** of stars.